Noodle

Story by
Munro Leaf

Pictures by
Ludwig Bemelmans

ARTHUR A. LEVINE BOOKS
An Imprint of Scholastic Inc.

Text copyright © 2006 by Munro Leaf. Originally published in 1937.
All rights reserved. Published by Arthur A. Levine Books, an imprint of Scholastic Inc., *Publishers since 1920.*
SCHOLASTIC and the LANTERN LOGO are trademarks and/or registered trademarks of Scholastic Inc. No part of this
publication may be reproduced, stored in a retrieval system, or transmitted in any form or by any means, electronic,
mechanical, photocopying, recording, or otherwise, without written permission of the publisher. For information
regarding permission, write to Scholastic Inc., Attention: Permissions Department, 557 Broadway, New York,
NY 10012. · Library of Congress Cataloging-in-Publication Data · Leaf, Munro, 1905– Noodle / by Munro Leaf &
Ludwig Bemelmans. p. cm. · Summary: When Noodle is granted a wish from the good dog fairy to be any size and
shape desired, he decides to remain Noodle. ISBN 0-590-04309-9 [1. Animals—Fiction. 2. Wishes—Fiction.
3. Fairies—Fiction. 4. Contentment—Fiction.] I. Bemelmans, Ludwig, 1898–1962, ill. II. Title. PZ10.3.L48No
2006 [Fic]—dc22 2005009993 · 10 9 8 7 6 5 4 3 2   · 06 07 08 09 10 · Book design by Richard Amari
First Arthur A. Levine Books printing, April 2006 · Printed in Singapore   46

DEDICATED WITH AFFECTION

TO

The REAL live NOODLE
whose superhuman common sense
inspired this story

This is the story of Noodle,

who was very long

        from

             front - - - -

                        to - - - - back,

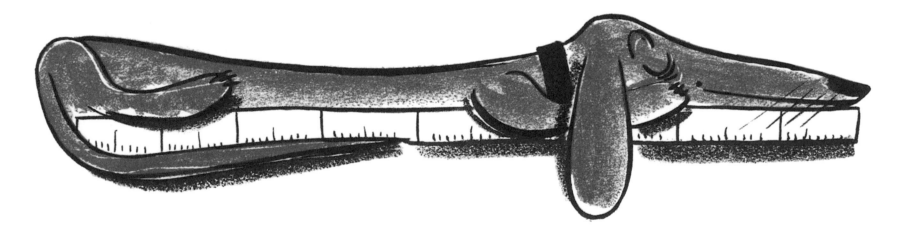

and very short

from

top
to
bottom.

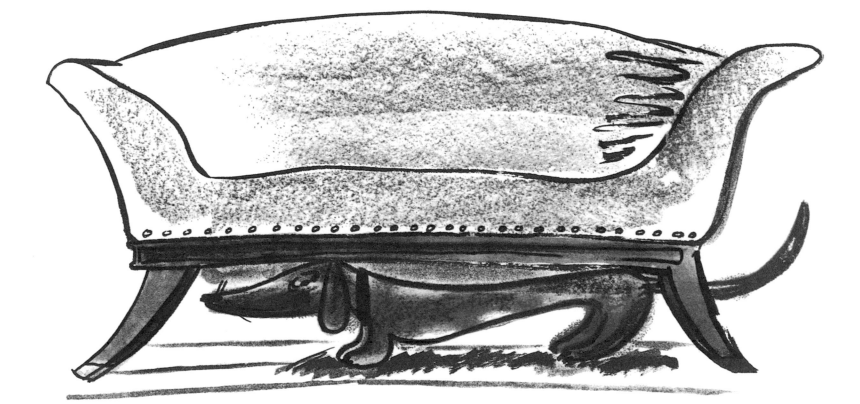

One day Noodle was digging in the garden. He liked to dig.

But he was so very long from front to back, and he was so very short from top to bottom, that it was hard for him.

The dirt he kicked up with his short front paws always hit him in the tummy.

This day, Noodle was digging deep into the ground because he was sure he smelled a bone.

All you could see from up top was his tail.

Just as he put the tip of his nose on the bone, he said out loud, "I do wish I could be some other size and shape. I could dig up this bone without so much work."

There was a whirr and a buzz and a flip-flap of wings behind him. Was it a bird?

Noodle did not look to see. He went on digging until he had worked the bone loose from the dirt and could carry it up to the top of the hole.

When he got to the top, he looked for the bird. But there instead was a little white dog with wings just like a bird's.

Noodle was surprised. "Who are you?" he said.

"I am the dog fairy," she said.

"Want part of this nice bone I just dug up?" said Noodle.

"No, thank you," said the dog fairy. "I just came to give you your wish."

"What wish?" said Noodle.

"The one you just made when you touched the tip of your nose to that wishbone," said the dog fairy.

"Why, so it is a wishbone!" said Noodle, looking at it carefully for the first time. "I forgot. What did I wish?"

"You wished you could be some other size and shape. Now here I am to give you your wish. What size and shape do you want to be?"

Noodle scratched his ear. "I don't know," he said. "May I have a little while to decide?"

"Yes," said the dog fairy, "but only until this afternoon. Then you must choose."

Off went the dog fairy with a whirr and a buzz and a flip-flap of wings.

And
        she
            took
                the
                    wishbone
                        with
                          her.

Noodle sat down to think. (He could always think better sitting down.) Wouldn't it be nice to be just the size and shape he wanted to be? But what size — and what shape? That was the question.

He thought and thought.

"I know what I will do!" he said. "I'll ask the animals at the zoo."

So off he went.

Pitter   patter.   pitter
          pitter   Patter   pitter.

(That was the sort of noise his feet made when he walked in a hurry.)

It was a nice day, and all the animals were outside. The first animal Noodle saw was a zebra.

"Hello, Mr. Zebra," said Noodle.

"Hello, Noodle," said Mr. Zebra. "What brings you to the zoo this fine day?"

"I have a question," said Noodle.

"Ask me," said the zebra. "I know a lot of answers."

"What is the best size and shape to be?" said Noodle.

"Oh, that's easy," said Mr. Zebra. "Just exactly my size and shape is the best one."

"Why?" said Noodle.

"I don't know why. It just is," said Mr. Zebra.

"Is it a good size for digging?" said Noodle.

"I really don't know," said Mr. Zebra. "I don't dig. But it is a fine size and shape for pulling a wagon."

"Oh," said Noodle, "do you pull wagons?"

"No," said Mr. Zebra. "But I'd like to."

"I don't think I would like to pull a wagon," said Noodle.
"But thank you for telling me.

Good-bye."

"You are welcome," said Mr. Zebra.

"Good-bye."

Noodle walked on until he came to a yard that had a deep pool of water in it. Noodle did not see anyone, but he could see some bubbles bubbling up out of the water. So he waited.

By and by there was a big "pfffffffffffff,"
                and up to the top came
                                  Mrs. Hippopotamus.

"Hello, Mrs. Hippopotamus," said Noodle.

"Hello, Noodle," said Mrs. Hippopotamus. "What brings you to the zoo this fine day?"

"I have a question," said Noodle.

"Ask me," said Mrs. Hippopotamus. "But you had better hurry. I'm going to the bottom again."

"What is the best size and shape to be?" said Noodle.

"I'll tell you when I come up," said Mrs. Hippopotamus.

And she took a big breath, and down to the bottom she went.

Noodle waited.

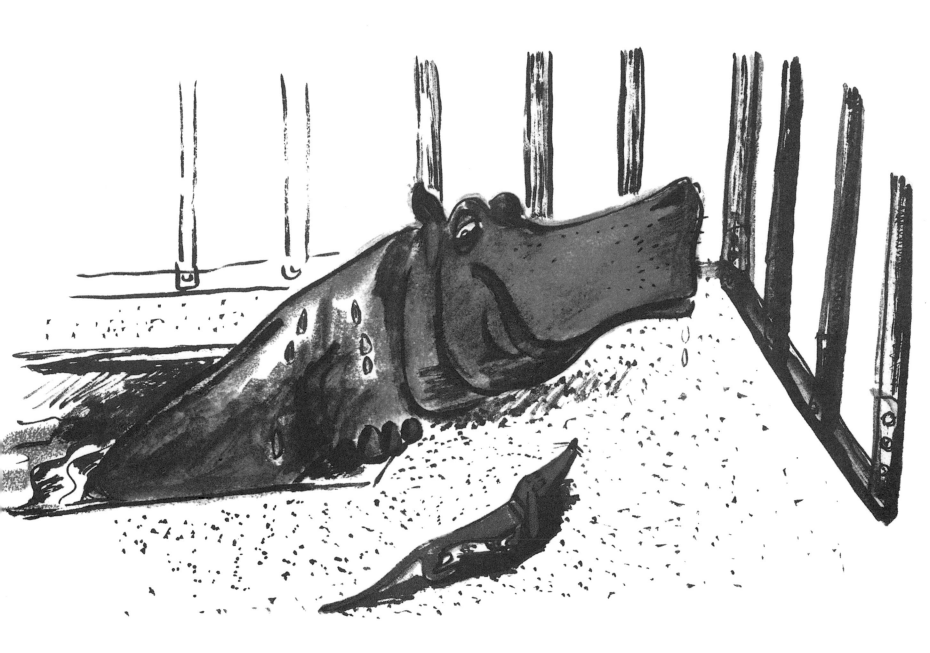

"Pffffffffffff," said Mrs. Hippopotamus, as she came up to the top again. "Just exactly my size and shape is the best one."

"Why?" said Noodle.

"I don't know why. It just is," said Mrs. Hippopotamus.

"Is it a good size for digging?" said Noodle.

"I don't think so," said Mrs. Hippopotamus. "But it is a fine size for going to the bottom of the pool."

"I don't think I would like that," said Noodle.
"But thank you, and

good-bye."

"You are quite welcome," said Mrs. Hippopotamus.
"Good-bye." And down she went to the bottom of the pool,

and up came the bubbles.

Noodle walked to the next yard. Way over in the corner was Miss Ostrich. Her head was in the sand.

Noodle shouted, "Oh, Miss Ostrich,

GOOD MORNING!"

Out popped Miss Ostrich's head, and she shook the sand out of her eyes.

"Oh, good morning, Noodle. How did you know I was here? I was hiding."

"Why, I saw all of you but your head," said Noodle.

"That's funny," said Miss Ostrich. "I didn't see you."

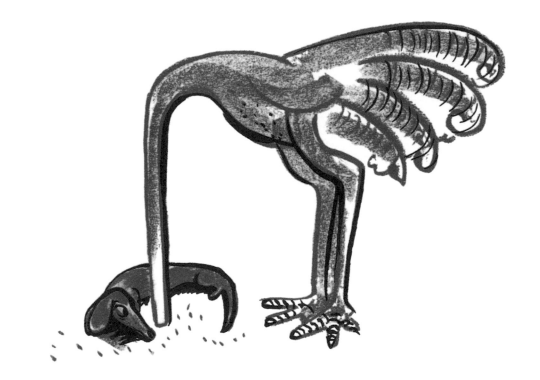

Noodle was going to ask Miss Ostrich what size and shape to be. But he decided not to. Miss Ostrich had her head in the sand again.

It was getting late, and Noodle was hungry. He hurried to the next yard. He had time to see one more animal before he went home to lunch.

In the next yard was Mr. Giraffe. He was busy nibbling the leaves from the top of a tree that grew over his fence.

"Good morning, Mr. Giraffe," said Noodle.

"Oh, good morning, Noodle," said Mr. Giraffe. "What brings you to the zoo so near to lunchtime?"

"I have a very important question," said Noodle. "And I am getting very hungry. Could you please answer me quickly?"

"Why certainly," said Mr. Giraffe. "I'll come right down."

And

he

leaned

way

down

with

his

neck

so Noodle could ask him.
"What is the best size and shape to be?" said Noodle.

"What a silly question!" said Mr. Giraffe. "Why, just the size and shape I am, of course."

"Oh," said Noodle. "Is it a good size for digging?"

"Of course not," said Mr. Giraffe. "But who wants to dig?"

"I do," said Noodle, "for good bones to eat."

"That's silly," said Mr. Giraffe. "Nice, tender green leaves from the tops of trees are best for eating. And my size and shape is just right for finding them."

"But I don't like to eat leaves," said Noodle, "and I am hungry right now. So thank you just the same, and

good-bye.

I am going home to lunch."

Mr. Giraffe said good-bye and stuck his neck back into the treetops.

Noodle went home and had his lunch.

After lunch, Noodle took a nap.

He was sound asleep until he heard a whirr and a buzz and a flip-flap of wings.

It was the dog fairy.

"I came back, just as I promised," she said.

"So I see," said Noodle, as he opened one eye. But he was too sleepy to keep it open.

"Have you decided what size and shape you wish to be?" said the dog fairy.

"Yes," said Noodle with his eyes closed.

"What size and shape do you wish to be?" asked the dog fairy.

"Just exactly

the

size

and

shape

I

am

right now,"

said Noodle. And he fell sound asleep.

"That is a very wise wish," said the dog fairy. And off she flew, with a whirr and a buzz and a flip-flap of wings.

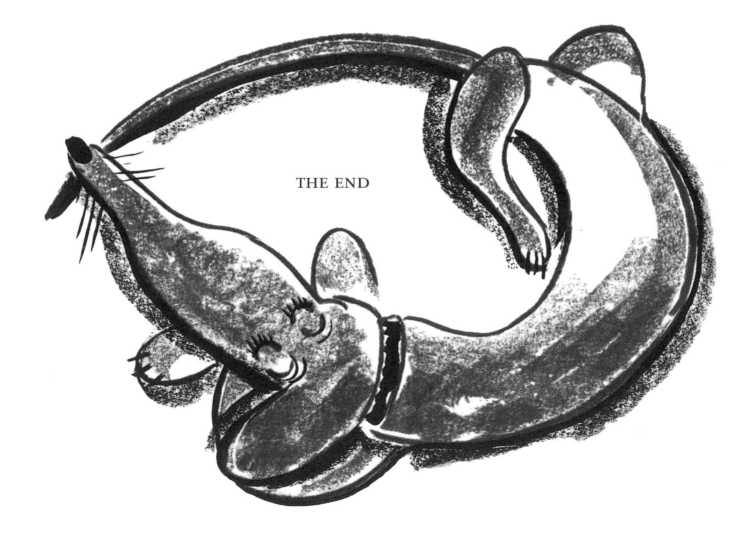

THE END